AUTO-B-GOOD™

MEAN 'OLE CRANKFENDER

A LESSON IN CARING

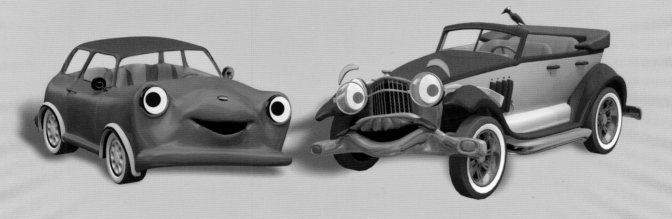

WRITTEN BY **PHILLIP WALTON**

ART BY RISING STAR STUDIOS

Free Activities, Coloring Pages, and Character Building Lessons Available Online!
www.risingstareducation.com

RISINGSTAR
STUDIOS

MEAN 'OLE CRANKFENDER: A Lesson in Caring

Written by Phillip Walton

A story based on the characters from the series Auto-B-Good™

ART & EDITORIAL DIRECTOR
Tom Oswald

CONTRIBUTING EDITOR
Nick Rogosienski

ADDITIONAL EDITING
Colleen Sexton

LEAD 3D ARTIST
Phillip Walton

ADDITIONAL ART
Drew Blom
Bruce Pukema

GRAPHIC DESIGNER AND LETTERER
Steve Plummer

COVER DESIGN
Steve Plummer

PRODUCTION MANAGER
Nick Rogosienski

PRODUCTION COORDINATOR
Mark Nordling

SPECIAL THANKS
John Richards
Linda Bettes
Barbara Gruener
Jack Currier

Printed in China:
Shenzhen Donnelley Printing Co., Ltd
Shenzhen, Guangdong Province, China
Completed: October 2009
P1_1009

Publisher's Cataloging-In-Publication Data
(Prepared by The Donohue Group, Inc.)
Walton, Phillip.
   Mean 'ole Crankfender : a lesson in caring / Phillip Walton ; art by Rising Star Studios, LLC.
      p. : ill. (holographic) ; cm. -- (Auto-B-Good)
   Summary: A story based on the characters from the series Auto-B-Good. After damaging his neighbor's birdhouse, EJ works off the debt by pulling weeds for "Mean 'Ole Crankfender." In the process, EJ learns what it means to be caring.
   Interest age level: 005-009.
   ISBN: 978-1-936086-04-7
1. Caring--Juvenile fiction. 2. Neighbors--Juvenile fiction. 3. Caring--Fiction. 4. Neighbors--Fiction. I. Rising Star Studios, LLC. II. Title.
PZ7.W3586 Me 2009
[E]

2009905757

A flying disc whizzed through the air. EJ jumped up and grabbed it. "Not bad!" his pal Johnny said. "Now send it back. And put some heat on it!"

"Get ready!" EJ shouted and wound up for a huge throw. He launched the disc into the air. It went wide and sailed away from Johnny.

"Dude!" yelled Johnny. "You were supposed to throw it **TO** me!" He raced after the disc.

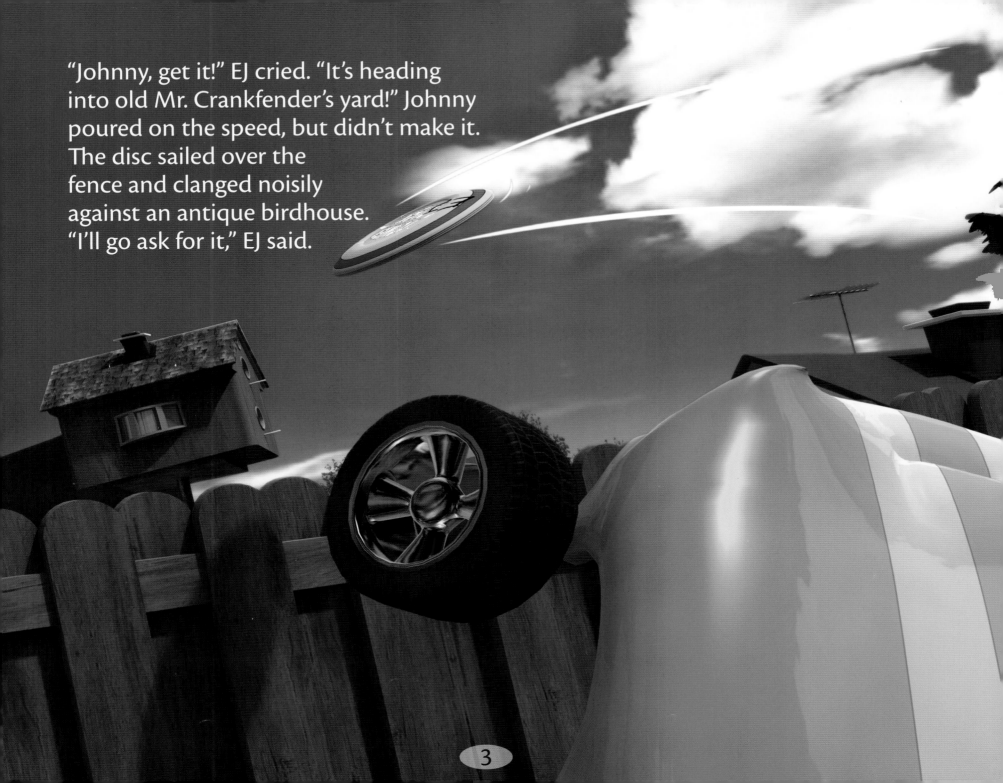

"Johnny, get it!" EJ cried. "It's heading into old Mr. Crankfender's yard!" Johnny poured on the speed, but didn't make it. The disc sailed over the fence and clanged noisily against an antique birdhouse. "I'll go ask for it," EJ said.

"I wouldn't do that if I were you," Johnny said. "I've heard that old Mr. Crankfender is the grumpiest car in the City of Auto! He keeps every toy that goes over his fence. He's using them to build a giant robot to take over the city."

"Really?" EJ asked.

Suddenly, the birdhouse tipped over and crashed to the ground.

"Oh man!" Johnny hooted. "You broke Crankfender's birdhouse. He's really going to blow a gasket!"

"But it was an accident," EJ said.

CRASH!

"What is going on out here!" an old car shouted.
His wheels creaked as he rolled out of his house.

"It's Crankfender!" Johnny said. "Let's get out of here."

Johnny and EJ raced away. They left Mr. Crankfender behind with the pieces of his broken birdhouse.

The next day, EJ heard a knock at his door. It was Franklin. "I understand you wrecked your neighbor's birdhouse," he said. "And you didn't even stay to apologize."

"What?" EJ said. "How did you know that?"

"Your name was on the flying disc," said Franklin.

"Oh, right," EJ sighed.

"I think you should buy Mr. Crankfender a new birdhouse," Franklin suggested. "It's the right thing to do."

9

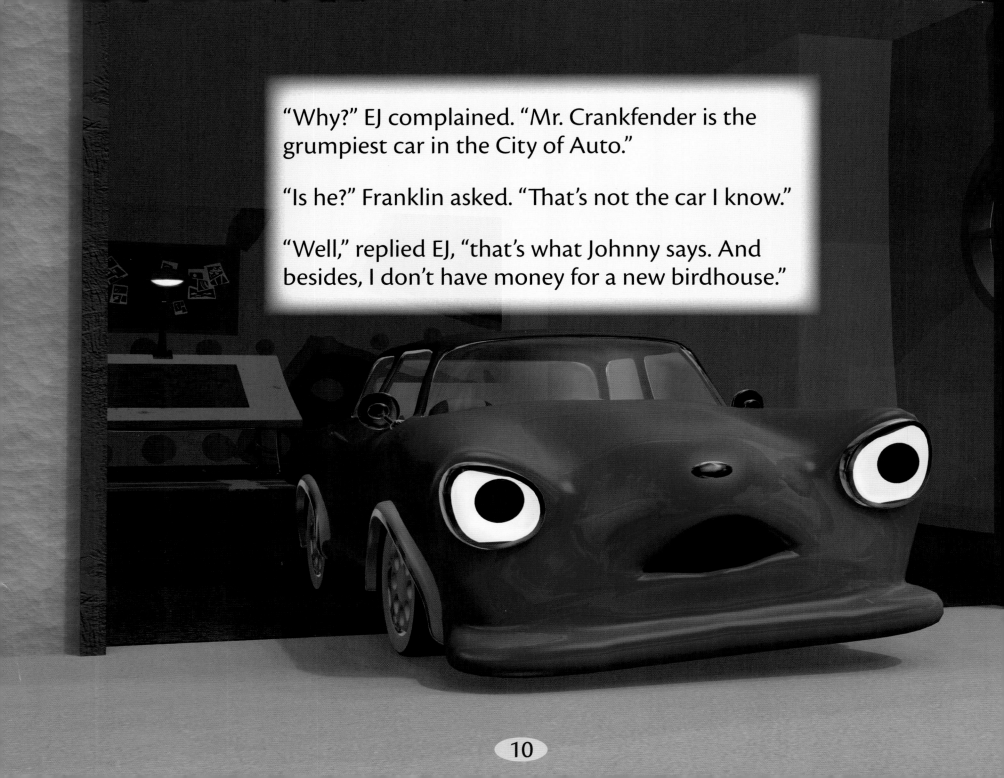

"Why?" EJ complained. "Mr. Crankfender is the grumpiest car in the City of Auto."

"Is he?" Franklin asked. "That's not the car I know."

"Well," replied EJ, "that's what Johnny says. And besides, I don't have money for a new birdhouse."

"Well Mr. Crankfender agreed that you can work off what you owe by helping him around the house," Franklin said.

"OK, fine," EJ agreed gloomily.

"Go to his house at eight o'clock tomorrow morning," Franklin said. "You'll finish when he thinks you've worked enough to pay for the birdhouse."

11

"You could offer him some extra help too, EJ," Franklin added. "Mr. Crankfender is getting on in years and needs someone to care for him."

"Care for him?" EJ asked. "Why would I do more than I have to? What's in it for me?"

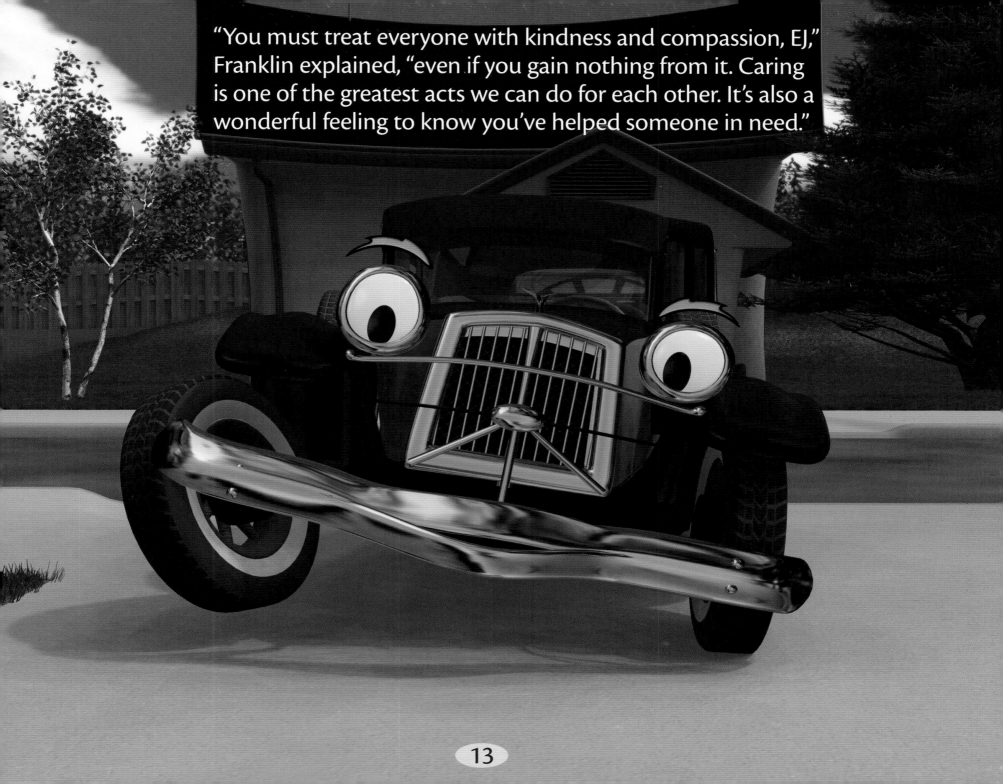

"You must treat everyone with kindness and compassion, EJ," Franklin explained, "even if you gain nothing from it. Caring is one of the greatest acts we can do for each other. It's also a wonderful feeling to know you've helped someone in need."

"And who knows? You might even learn a few things from Mr. Crankfender," Franklin said as he was leaving. EJ wasn't so sure about that.

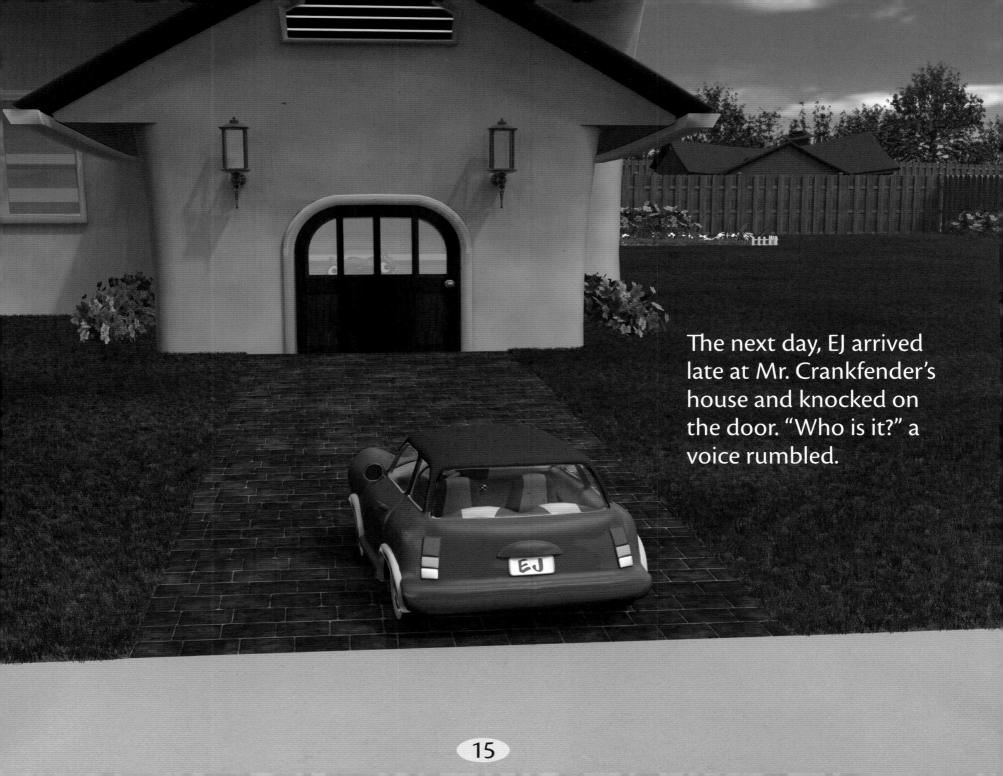

The next day, EJ arrived late at Mr. Crankfender's house and knocked on the door. "Who is it?" a voice rumbled.

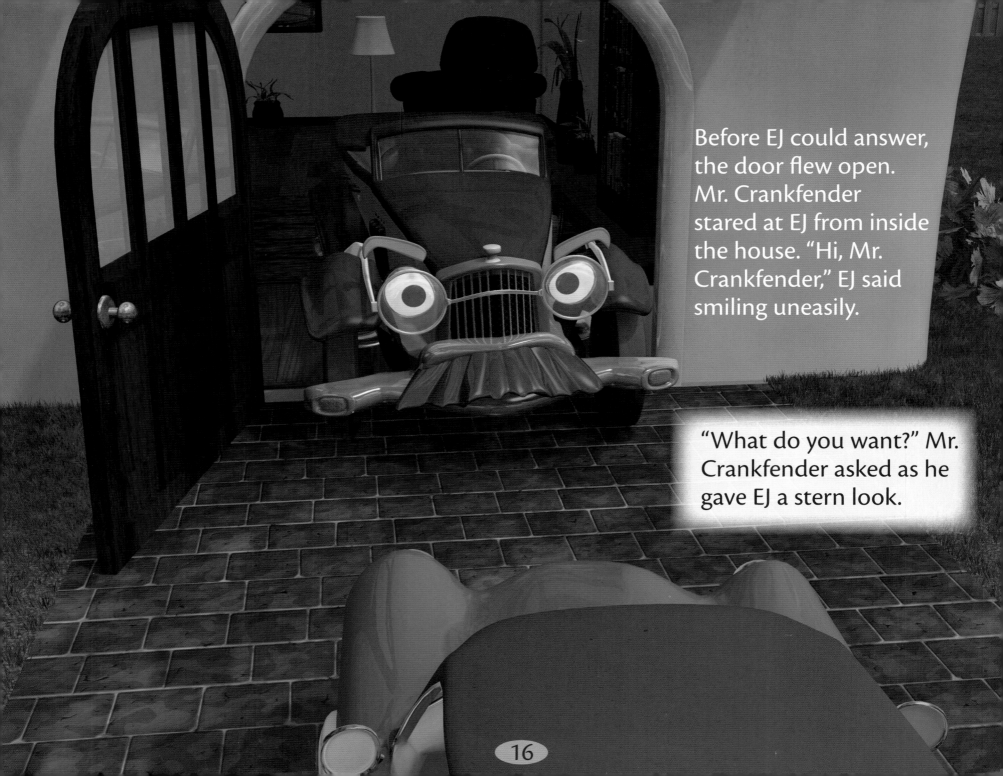

Before EJ could answer, the door flew open. Mr. Crankfender stared at EJ from inside the house. "Hi, Mr. Crankfender," EJ said smiling uneasily.

"What do you want?" Mr. Crankfender asked as he gave EJ a stern look.

16

EJ gulped. "I'm EJ, sir. Franklin said I'm supposed to do some work for you."
"Ah! You're the kid who wrecked my birdhouse! Well DJ, you're late. We have
work to do. Let's go," the old car said.

"It's EJ, sir," EJ tried to say. But Mr. Crankfender was already driving toward the backyard.

18

"We're gonna start by pickin' weeds in Laura's garden," Mr. Crankfender said.

"Yes, sir," EJ replied glumly. EJ groaned when he saw the rough and overgrown garden. But he also noticed beautiful flowers poking out among all the weeds.

For several hours, EJ and Mr. Crankfender pulled weeds. They worked side by side in silence.

"Watch those geraniums, DJ," Mr. Crankfender said as EJ almost backed over a white bloom. Mr. Crankfender pointed to a bright orange flower.

"These used to be my prize-winning zinnias. I took them to the flower show every year. Nowadays, it's just too hard for me to take care of them."

21

"That's too bad," EJ thought and remembered the time he helped Franklin at the flower show. EJ silently went back to work. He just wanted to finish weeding and get out of there.

22

"Will that be all, Mr. Crankfender?" EJ asked later that afternoon. "I finished weeding around the yellow and white flowers."

"Daisies," Mr Crankfender said and frowned. "You can go for today. There's more to do tomorrow, DJ. And show up on time!"

"Tomorrow? But—" The old car
gave him a stern look.

"Mean 'ole Crankfender,"
EJ mumbled quietly as he drove off.

25

EJ returned bright and early the next day to help Mr. Crankfender.

"Got here on time. That's more like it," Mr. Crankfender said.

"What are we doing today, sir?" EJ asked.

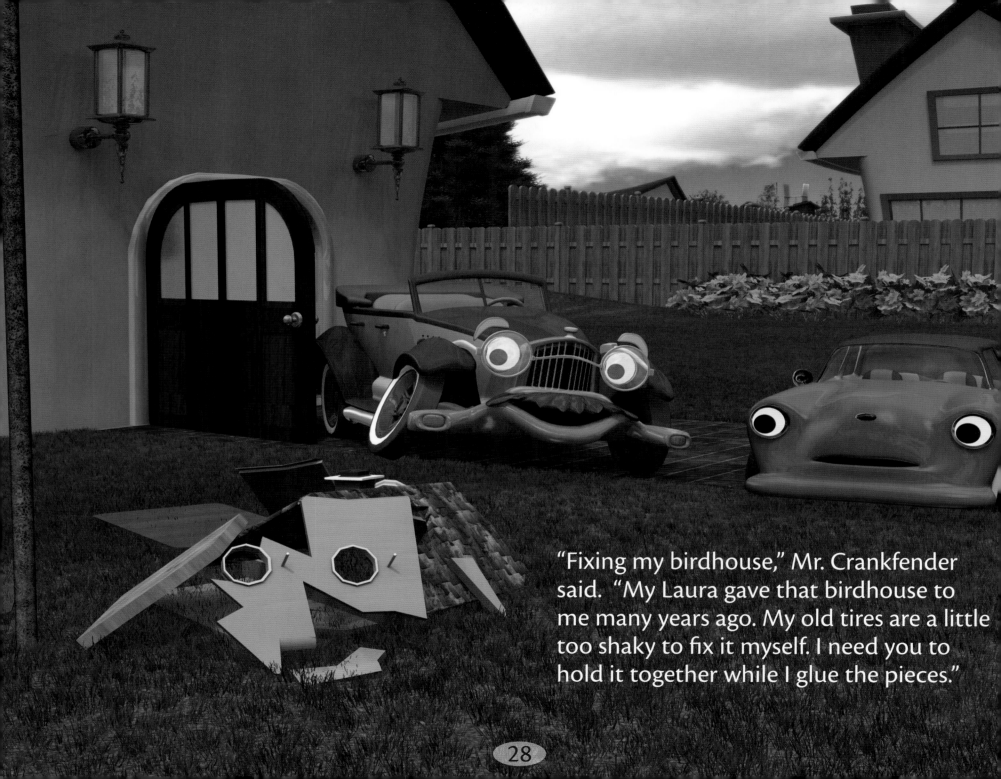

"Fixing my birdhouse," Mr. Crankfender said. "My Laura gave that birdhouse to me many years ago. My old tires are a little too shaky to fix it myself. I need you to hold it together while I glue the pieces."

While they worked, Mr. Crankfender told EJ about the birds that lived in the neighborhood.

EJ noticed a bright red feather on the ground. "What kind of bird is this one from, Mr. Crankfender?" EJ asked.

"Oh, that's from a ruby-backed thrush warbler," Mr. Crankfender said. "They've nested in this birdhouse for as long as I can remember. Laura used to love their song."

"She doesn't like it anymore?" EJ asked.

30

"No, DJ," Mr. Crankfender said sadly. "My Laura isn't with us anymore."

"Oh," EJ said. He suddenly felt bad. "I'm really sorry for breaking your birdhouse and running away. It wasn't very nice."

"Well, you didn't know this old birdhouse was so important to me. But I'm glad you're here to set things right," Mr. Crankfender said.

It wasn't long before the bird house was all glued together and as good as new. They paused to look at their handiwork.

"I think we did a pretty good job." EJ smiled, suddenly feeling wonderful.

"You're right, DJ. I'd say we make a pretty good team."

33

"Actually, my name is EJ."

"Oh, sorry about that," Mr. Crankfender chuckled. "I thought I heard the other kids calling you DJ. I guess I was wrong."

"You can't always trust what you hear from the other kids," EJ said with a grin.

"Well EJ, I think you've worked off what you owe. You can go now if you want," Mr. Crankfender said with a sad smile.

"Thanks," EJ said. And then he stopped. He looked up and saw a little red bird land on the birdhouse perch.

"Look, Mr. Crankfender! Is that a red-backed thistle thingy?" EJ asked excitedly.

"Well, would you look at that! It certainly is, EJ," Mr. Crankfender said and then pulled out a bucket of birdseed. "Here, EJ, toss some of this on the ground."

A second ruby-backed thrush warbler flew down to the birdseed. Several other birds followed. "Wow!" EJ cried. "That's cool!"

"It is cool, EJ," Mr. Crankfender said. "My Laura always said how important it is that everyone take care of each other. I guess that's why I like to take care of the little birds."

"I bet that's what Franklin was talking about," EJ thought to himself. "It feels good to be caring toward others."

"Mr. Crankfender?" EJ said. "I would really like to help you get your zinnias ready for the flower show this year."

"EJ! That would be wonderful!
Thank you!" Mr. Crankfender said
and smiled broadly.

41

EJ smiled too. He couldn't wait to tell Johnny that all the crazy talk about Mr. Crankfender wasn't true.

EJ was just about ready to leave for the day, when Mr. Crankfender handed him his flying disc. "Here EJ, I want you to have this back. You've done a good job."

"Besides, I don't really need any more toys. The giant robot I'm building to take over the city is coming along just fine."

"What!" EJ gasped.

Mr. Crankfender winked, and they
both had a good long laugh.